Dillan McMillan

PLEASE
Eat Your Peas!

by **David Schneider** • illustrated by **Jeff Shelly**

All About Kids Publishing

Library of Congress Cataloging-in-Publication Data
LCCN: 2007031510
Schneider, David A., 1960-
Dillan McMillan, Please Eat Your Peas / by David Schneider ; illustrated by
Jeff Shelly.

p. cm.

Summary: Everyone, from the neighbors to the President to aliens from outer space, tries
to persuade Dillan McMillan to eat his peas, but his little sister is the one who solves
the problem.
ISBN-13: 978-0-9744446-4-2 (alk. paper)
ISBN-10: 0-9744446-4-2 (alk. paper)
[1. Food habits--Fiction. 2. Peas--Fiction. 3. Behavior--Fiction.] I. Shelly, Jeff, ill. II. Title.
PZ7.S36235Di 2007

[E]--dc22
Printed by RR Donnelley Asia Printing Solutions
Limited in Dongguan, Guangdong, China
30 29 28 27 26 25 24 23 22 21 20 19 18 17 16 15 14 13 12 11 10 9 8 7 6 5 4 3 2 1

All About Kids Publishing
7680 Monterey St. #307
Gilroy, CA 95020

www.allaboutkidspub.com

To Cheryl for the encouragement;

to Anna and Emma for the inspiration;

to all three for their love.

They were tiny, roly-poly, soft, green, warm, steamy, bumpy, buttery...and sitting on Dillan McMillan's plate.

His Mother said sweetly,
"Dillan McMillan, please eat your peas.
You had them just last week
Remember? You liked them."
She promised him dessert.

But Dillan McMillan would not eat his peas.

His father said firmly, "Dillan McMillan, please eat your peas. Peas make you grow up to be big and strong, You want to be big and strong, don't you? If you eat them, I'll give you a quarter."

But Dillan McMillan would not eat his peas.

A few moments later Dillan's grandmother stopped by to see him. She said, "Dillan McMillan, please eat your peas. If you do, Grandma will take you to the park tomorrow. We'll get an ice cream, too."

But Dillan McMillan, would not eat his peas.

Dillan's best friend came over. He dared Dillan McMillan to eat his peas. He double dared him. He triple dared him. He said, "Dillan McMillan, please eat your peas. I'll give you my special autographed baseball."

But Dillan McMillan would not eat his peas.

Soon, everyone in the neighborhood heard about Dillan.
All the neighbors gathered in front of Dillan's house. They
began to cheer, "PLEASE, PLEASE, PLEASE! EAT YOUR PEAS,
PEAS, PEAS! We'll buy you a brand new bike. Just eat one
forkful! Or even one little pea!"

But Dillan McMillan would not eat his peas.

Then, the police came to control the crowd. There were police cars in Dillan's front yard. They had flashing red and blue lights. A helicopter hovered over his house. A policewoman came into the kitchen. She said, "Dillan McMillan, please eat your peas. If you do, I'll let you ride in my car, and you can turn on the siren, as much as you want!"

But Dillan McMillan would not eat his peas.

Soon, TV reporters showed up. "What a story!" they said. They told the whole country about the stubborn little boy who refused to eat his peas. Telephone calls came in from all over. Everyone said, "Dillan McMillan, please eat your peas. We'll give you a dog...or a cat...or how about a horse?"

But Dillan McMillan would not eat his peas.

Then the President appeared on TV. He said, "Dillan McMillan, please eat your peas. Girls and boys all over the country won't eat theirs until you do. Moms and dads everywhere are getting very angry. If you eat your peas, you can visit me at the White House. That's in Washington. And, I'll give you a medal!"

But Dillan McMillan would not eat his peas.

Just then, a spaceship landed in Dillan's back yard. Out came little green pea people. They said "Little earthling, Dillan McMillan, please eat your peas. We will give you a ride in our spaceship. You can see outer space and walk on the moon. You can come to our planet where the mountains are made of chocolate."

But Dillan McMillan would not eat his peas.

The kitchen became very noisy and crowded. No one knew what to do. Everyone was shouting at each other.

Finally, Dillan's little sister got up from the table.

She made her way through the crowd of neighbors and
police officers and reporters and little green pea people.

She went up to the refrigerator.

She opened the door.

She took out the ketchup.

And Dillan McMillan ate his peas.

David Schneider

grew up in upstate New York. He is now

an attorney residing in Jupiter, Florida, with

his wife and two daughters, none of whom

eat peas, and a dachshund who probably

would. *Dillan McMillan* is his

first picture book.

Jeff Shelly

began working as an animator
and illustrator in New York City.

His career with the Walt Disney Company
brought him to Los Angeles where he was
Director of Character Art for Imagineering-Disney
Parks, Experiences and Consumer Products for 28
years. His work can be seen on product lines developed
for Coach, Apple, Pottery Barn Kids
and Shinola to name a few.

He has worked for various animation studios
and his illustrations can be seen in children's
books, magazines, educational publications
and advertising.

Jeff works out of his studio in the
Hollywood Hills illustrating,
writing and painting.